Mimi's Book of Counting

Emma Chichester Clark

Charlesbridge

"You are my little dumpling!" said Grandma.

"How many dumplings do you have?"
asked Mimi.

"You are my one and only dumpling!" said Grandma.

1

"How many jars of honey do I have?"
"Two!" said Mimi.

"And three cans of chicken soup!"

"And how many oranges?" asked Grandma.
"One, two, three, four!" said Mimi.

"Five fingers on each hand!" said Mimi.

"And five toes on each foot!" said Grandma.

"And look at those!" said Grandma. "How many flowers in that big pot?"

"Six flowers," said Mimi, "and one bee!"

"I hope you're not going to leave all those beans!" said Grandma.

7

"One, two, three, four, five, six, seven . . .
all gone!" said Mimi.

"I've never seen so many boats!" said Grandma.

"Eight boats,
one duck,
and one helicopter!"
said Mimi.

"Let's read your favorite book,"
said Grandma.

"I have nine!" said Mimi.
"Just one," said Grandma.

"There are lots of teddies under your bed!" said Grandma.

"One, two, three, four, five, six, seven, eight, nine . . .

. . . ten!" said Mimi.
"And one book, and one
Grandma, and one dumpling!"